I0818646

Fly By Night

Fly By Night

Arthur Dekker Savage

ÆGYPAN PRESS

This text from *IF Worlds of Science Fiction,* May, 1954.

Special thanks to Greg Weeks, Mary Meehan, and the Online Distributed Proofreading Team (which can be found at http://www.pgdp.net).

Fly By Night
A publication of
ÆGYPAN PRESS

www.aegypan.com

A young man and a young woman alone on the first over-the-moon ship. The world cheered them as the most romantic adventurers in all history. Do-gooders decried them as immoral stunters. Gaunt, serious militarists pronounced them part of the most crucial experiment ever undertaken. . . .

The general introduced them in the ship's shadow, a trim lieutenant, a clean-cut major. "You probably already think of each other as Carol and Ken. At any rate, there are no two people in the world who have heard as much about each other without previously meeting."

She offered her hand and he took it, held it for a long moment while their eyes locked. "Hello, Carol," he said warmly. "I'd have known you from your pictures." And he realized as never before what a poor substitute were the hoarded scraps of paper.

"Hello – Ken." A smile made her face radiant. "I've sort of studied your pictures too."

Ken turned his eyes to the crowd – a roaring, cheering multitude surrounding the poised rocket ship here on the California desert in this zero hour. To certain harried physicists and engineers, it was a moment promising paramount achievement. To romanticists of 1966, watching their video screens avidly, it was fulfillment of their most sensual dreams: a beautiful girl being given wholly and unreservedly to a handsome young man; the flight around the moon was merely an added fillip. To a few gaunt military psychologists it was the end of a long nightmare of protests by women's clubs, demonstrations by national female societies and actual attempts at murder by fanatical blue-noses; and a mere beginning of the most crucial experiment ever undertaken – which *had* to be a success.

Suddenly Ken was angry at the knowing looks from the throng's nearest ranks. While the general continued his prepared speech into the mike, focus of the hollow, hungry eyes of the video cameras, Ken pulled Carol to his side and held her with an arm about her waist, glaring when the crowd murmured and the cameras swung their way again. He had not questioned the actions of the military, of the world, before. But now – a public spectacle –

During the years of rigorous, specialized training almost from childhood they had kept him away from Carol, teasing him – it was the only word that now occurred to his mind – with the dangled promise of her presence on the flight. They had let him see her pictures – intimate, almost-nude photos harvested by the gossip columnists, snaps of her glory in bathing attire as she lounged by a swimming pool.

Swimming. Since he had been selected as a boy, every free afternoon he had been made to swim, swim, swim – developing the long, smooth muscles they wanted him to have. It had been, he knew, the same with Carol.

Had they taunted her with his pictures too? Had she responded by wanting him, loving him, longing for him? How did she feel about their first moment together being shared by the greedy eyes of continents?

The President was speaking now, rolling sonorous sentences into the mike, words which would officially sanction this unorthodox act of the military, which would justify the morally unprecedented dispensing of maid to man without benefit of – anything. Because the psychologists had wanted it that way. Ken leaned down to whisper in her ear, "I wish I could get you inside the ship."

She looked at him with sudden coolness. "Impatient, Major?" She turned away quickly and he could feel her body stiffen.

Had he said something wrong? Or – the new thought was jarring disharmony: did he represent the end of this girl's – *his* girl's – hopes for a conventional, happy marriage? Did she think him the altar of sacrifice, whereupon she would accrue the moralist's scorn and, tomorrow, attract only the lecherous? Or was it just an act? What, besides ship and instrument operation, had they taught her?

Grimly he listened to the President, who was then extolling their merits as though – well, as though they were some sort of laboratory specimens. ". . . acute hearing, 20/10 vision . . . perfect health . . . highest combination of intelligence and fast physical reactions . . . exceptional bravery and loyalty." Cheers. ". . . intensive training . . . youngest to receive their military ranks . . . expert pilots . . . *fittest humans for this attempt.*"

Stubbornly, Ken continued to hold her waist. He watched the sun sneak around one stubby wing of the *Latecomer.* He'd need those glinting wings to land. Land? What were the actual odds against circling the moon and landing again on earth? That phase – and a lot of others – had never been discussed. The speeches were over and he put the thought from his mind. They were extending the mike to him, waiting for his farewell – or his last words?

Abruptly, ignoring the mike, he swung Carol up the ramp and crawled in through the port behind her.

In the narrow confines she slipped out of her uniform. She glanced at him once, quickly, then cast down her eyes. "You don't have to look, you know."

There was a hurt in his throat. "I want to look, Carol. I don't ever want to stop looking at you. I –" He choked off, tore his eyes from her and hurriedly began to get out of his uniform.

Hidden from the spectators outside, they divested themselves of all but filmy, clinging, chemically inert garb. Carol's body was sheathed in a kind of sarong. Ken wore a short, kiltlike affair. They pulled on soft, tough-soled sandals. The medics had insisted on this specific attire, but the psychologists had planned it that way. Their discarded clothing was dropped into a basket. Ken shoved it out the port, down the ramp, slammed and bolted the hatch. Then he stared at it. Clamped to the inner side were two knives: one was about the length of a bayonet, shaped like a saber; the other was half that length, and straight. Both were sheathed, with belts wrapped around checkered handles.

All his official instructions flashed through his head in an instant. All the technical data, instrument operation, procedures, emergency measures. There had never been mention of knives. Except – of course. Survival training. If he were unable to bring the ship to its proper destination, was forced down in uninhabited territory, a knife would be essential equipment. But so would a gun, fishing tackle, matches, clothing. . . .

The ship's radio said, "Fourteen minutes to takeoff."

Ken flung himself on the couch. Carol moved in quietly beside him.

"You understand, Carol," he said, "you're to touch no controls unless I'm unable to."

"Yes."

"You'll handle the cameras only, but you'll keep reminding me of every step to be taken, as though I'd forgotten, and make sure I answer sensibly each time."

"Yes, Ken."

Yes, *Ken.* A pulse throbbed in his temple.

They watched the crowd on the screen – scattered now, far from that area below and behind the ship which would be washed in radiation. They listened to the radio calling off the minutes before departure. Ken kept his thoughts on the structure of the space vessel, similar in many ways to vastly cheaper atmosphere models he and Carol had flown – separately – for hundreds of training hours. Behind them, and lining the inner hull, was a light, spongy wall protecting them from the atomic converters aft. The surrounding couch could be regulated to form a resilient cocoon during high-G acceleration and deceleration, or during periods of weightlessness. Forward were the controls, instruments and hooded viewport.

Escape velocity was not needed to pull away from gravity. With atomic engines and the new, low-mass shielding, fuel quantity was a problem of dollars only – and none had been spared for this voyage. The psychologists had seen to that.

"Eight minutes to take-off."

He started the atomic reactors, a mighty purring here in the sealed cabin. Gently, watching the instruments, he tested bow and stern rockets, matching fore and aft forces delicately, tentatively increasing stern thrust until the craft barely stirred in its silicone-greased, magnetized launching rack.

"Two minutes to take-off."

They placed their faces against soft masks in the couch, down through which they could watch the instruments, in a mirror, the video screen and bow viewport. The couch encompassed them, their arms in padded slots reaching to the controls.

". . . thirty-four, thirty-three, thirty-two, thirty-one. . . ."

Thunder hammered at their ears. The couch squeezed them as the *Latecomer* shot beyond its ramp, increased its velocity. Ken gripped a lever which cut in the autopilot to take them beyond atmosphere, beyond gravity.

Ken unhooded the viewport, leaving covered only that section which blocked a tiny blinding sun. They stared into an utter, absolute ebony that suddenly seemed to be straining against the thick canopy, mocking the dim lights of the compartment. For many hours now, nothing to do but wait and watch, make occasional control corrections.

He caused the couch to relax, offered Carol a water sausage. They had eaten nothing, and drunk but sparingly, since twenty-four hours before take-off. Her hand touched his as she took the container. It was like an electric shock, and his heart thudded. Deliberately, he brushed his fingers over hers, clasped her wrist, looking at her.

She became motionless. Then she looked up at him, lingeringly. Her lips parted.

The pressure within him mounted. Almost reverently he reached for her – then stopped when tears formed in her eyes. He drew back, uncomprehending. Could desire be coupled with sorrow? Or was he merely reading desire into some emotion not remotely connected with passion? She had been given to him without reservation, but he could not bring himself to take her unwillingly. The difference, he realized, between love and lust – damn the psychologists. He let out his breath, fumbled in a small plastic box near the controls, dug out several nutriment bars. He handed a couple to Carol without looking at her and munched unhappily at the chocolate-flavored ration.

They watched the blackness of space for hours. The stars appeared as bright glowing blobs sunk dismally far into the heavy depths of some Stygian jelly. It was a time to be savoring the first experience of man beyond his mortal sphere, but Ken stared unseeingly, his mind dulled, vacant with indecision and disillusion that was almost a physical hurt. The zest of adventure, in the midst of adventure, was throttled before it saw life. The sustaining dreams of training and preparation were dusty misery. Robotically, he watched the instruments, occasionally made microscopic adjustments. Carol's hands, close to his, infrequently changed camera settings.

Unexpectedly the radio sounded. Ken tuned to maximum volume, strained to hear the muted words. It was a moment before he realized they were drawling, abnormally slow, like one of the old spring-wound phonographs running down. When he caught it, the message stunned him.

"*Late-comm-merr* pers-sonn-nell. Re-turnn noww, noww, noww. Emerr-genn-cy orr-derr of the Prezz-zident. *Llate-comm-merr* pers-sonn-nell. . . ."

He listened to it twice more before silencing the radio. Turn back? Now? He looked at Carol. She returned his stare, drawing her arms up out of the slots and leaning on her elbows, frowning in puzzlement. Her breasts were pendent promises of – further disappointment? Were both love and life to be reduced, in a day, to twin voids of defeat? Love was Carol and life was a successful flight around the moon.

Discipline kept his act just short of viciousness as he slapped the controls back to manual. Grimly he silenced the stern rockets, cut in the bow units slowly. The flight was to have been a loop "over" the moon, almost intersecting its orbit at the precise time it swung ponderously by. What possible emergency could have arisen?

Ken couldn't remember just when the fear had started – maybe on the way outward, now that he thought of it: the feeling of deep depression. They were in free fall, weightless, the couch adjusted to keep them floating within a few inches of its confines. The brilliant, abandoned moon had just swung behind its big-sister world, the glaring furnace of Sol was still thwarted by a section of bow hood.

He felt the fear mount – little tugging fingers frantically at work within his chest. The blue sphere of Earth seemed to recede in the black muck, although he knew it was only an optical effect of space – of the vast, scornful emptiness in which the stars were but helpless, hopelessly enmeshed droplets of dross.

He shivered involuntarily. With the movement he touched the side of the couch and rebounded against Carol.

She screamed.

He stared at her, his fear mounting swiftly through panic to abject, uncaring terror. Carol had drawn herself up into a knot, the fetal position of infantile regression; her eyes were wide, unseeing, her mouth open in the scream that was now soundless.

Ken felt his mind brinking on madness. He continued to stare in a terrified frenzy until, from some tiny nook of sanity deep inside him, came the realization that this was Carol beside him – Carol, who was his, who needed him. . . .

He fought. He staggered up from depths of bleak despair, aided by that deep-rooted male instinct which rouses raging fury at danger to his beloved. The innate protective impulse was heightened, strengthened by that emotional desire which is strongest at first contact, undiluted by familiarity and the consequent dissolution of ideals. The prime strength of manhood blasted in a coruscating mental flare against the forces of darkness and the unknown. Tenderly, he encircled her floating body with his arms and drew her close. He soothed her as one might a baby.

Slowly her eyes came back from horrific infinity. Slowly they focused on his. And then, comprehension returned, she pressed tightly against him, clung to him, sobbing with the remnant fear of fear remembered.

He talked to her for an hour, caressing, reassuring, until her responses were normal beyond any doubt. Then he told her he loved her.

She raised her head from where it was burrowed against his chest. "*Love* me, Ken? Love *me*?"

He blinked in astonishment. "Of course I love you. It seems like I've always loved you. I tried to tell you. I –"

But she was crying again, shaking her head a little, saying, "Ken, Ken," over and over.

This time he continued to hold her intimately close. "What's the matter? Anything wrong with love?"

"But Ken – you could have any girl in the world!"

"Me? Where'd you get that idea?"

"Why, everyone knows the story of your training, and what it was for. The swoon clubs must have sent you tons of letters!"

"I never got any."

"Censors?"

He shrugged. "Could be. I used to drive myself nuts thinking of all the guys you must be going out with. Your story was spread around just as much as mine."

"They picked my few escorts with care. I used to lie awake thinking of you running around with hundreds of girls."

Ken snorted. "The army kept me too busy. I went out with a few, but I never loved anybody but you. Hell, I'm only nineteen, you know."

She nodded, her eyes bright with happiness. She was a year younger. Then her words came in a flood. "I couldn't believe you'd love me. They told me I was to go with you and do anything you said – anything. No explanation, but I knew what they meant and I agreed because you were doing such a great thing for the world and – I wanted you too. But I thought you'd just want me for the trip, and afterward you'd go back to your other girls, and –"

He kissed her. Again. And again. Surely there never was, never could be, a greater delight embracing than in the floating, heady, free fall of null-G. Certainly the psychologists knew no other method of retaining sanity in the cruelly endless jet pit engulfing the stars. Which was why they had planned it that way.

Well out of atmosphere he began to brake skillfully, easing the craft into an orbital arc that would later be changed to a descending spiral. Biting into rarified air, he adjusted the hull heat distributor, cut in the refrigeration unit, increased oxygen a trifle. He removed a small envelope from its taped position on a panel and opened it to read his landing instructions. Then he looked questioningly at Carol.

"Southwest Oregon. The Oregon Caves National Monument. We're to go in on a beacon signal."

"You don't suppose they want us to show survival ability?"

"On a deal like this? No, something's haywire here. First, there's not a strip that'll take the *Latecomer* for at least a hundred miles around, and the only road into the area twists like a snake. This baby wasn't built with a chute, either. Second, it's only about ten miles from some ranches, even if there's no one at the château, so it wouldn't be a survival problem." He dropped the craft's nose a few more degrees.

"Are there anymore instructions?"

"Must be." He unfolded the slip. "'Abandon ship immediately upon landing. Enter bronze portal to Caves with all possible haste. Look for inscribed square beside door, with a slot at each corner. Activate door as follows: simultaneously insert curved blade of longer knife entirely in upper left-hand slot, and straight blade of shorter knife entirely in lower right-hand slot. Extreme emergency. Memorize and destroy these orders.'" Carol hadn't seen the knives.

They lay in stunned silence until she gasped, "But, Ken – this means they *knew* about the emergency before we took off!"

He nodded grimly. "We were never supposed to reach the moon." He crumpled the paper, thrust it into his mouth and chewed on it awhile, then slipped it into the waste disposal unit. "Well, we'll pick up the beacon and buzz the Caves area for possibilities. There was nothing said about making radio contact, so we'll just listen in. Want to take over the radio on the way down?" He forced the *Latecomer* into as tight a spiral as he dared. The wings were still useless here in the ionosphere.

Carol turned on the receiver, dialed expectantly. "Ken – the whole band is silent!"

"Take it easy, Lieutenant honey – we're barely through the F_2 layer."

But all bands remained dead except for sun static. Rockets chattering for a 2G brake and directional control, they plunged through the F_1 stratum, losing Sol behind the eastern rim of Terra. Down, down for dim countless minutes, through the thin ionization of E, past the lowest ranges of auroras and noctilucent clouds and below the ozone layer. Still no signals of any kind on any frequency.

At last Ken leveled off in the troposphere, at an altitude of five miles. A placid, swollen sun rode into view while they flashed west-ward over the Atlantic in a straight and lowering course that would take them over New York. The momentous – even though aborted – flight was over. Each tiniest mechanism of the *Latecomer* had functioned perfectly. Ken took a deep breath at the sheer pleasure of normal gravity. Man held the key to the planets, at least – if the psychologists could figure some way to nullify the soul-shattering fear imbued by deep space. Or had he and Carol reached the maximum distance life could tolerate? Was that the foreseen emergency, withheld from them lest it sap their carefully-nurtured morale? He felt a vague, gnawing worry about the silence of earth's transmitters.

New York would supply the answer. Over New York the cacaphony of blaring broadcasts would practically tear the receivers from their moorings.

And New York did yield an answer – of sorts. With Long Island in visual range, and not a sound or a picture on any wave length which Carol's flying fingers tuned in at maximum volume, Ken dipped below legal ceiling to drag the city.

Then his reactions galvanized him to motion of a speed outstripping his thoughts. Hardly hearing Carol's gasp of dismay, he snapped the coccoon tight about them like a sprung trap, blasted the ship's nose to a skidding vertical and spurted away from the yawning craters of New York City at five Gs.

He leveled off in ozone over Canada and relaxed the couch. Unbelievingly, he looked at Carol. She looked back at him, wide-eyed.

"Listen, Carol – we can't both be crazy the same way. You tell me exactly what you saw."

"Well – everything had been bombed."

"What else?"

"There – there wasn't any movement or people or –"

"What else."

"There – oh, Ken, there were *trees growing in the craters!"*

Some of the tenseness left his features. "Okay, honey. Now we know a little bit. The war came and went and there's not an active transmitter in the world. Somebody knew it was coming, even before we left, so they want us to land at a hideout in Oregon. There'll be a landing strip there – they've had more than a month to build it since I was at the Caves, and it only took a day for the whole war, for the radiation to clear up – and for twenty – maybe fifty-year-old trees to grow!" His ending sarcasm was directed at himself; youth angers at the spur of illogicalness.

Carol pressed his shoulder and kissed him. "Darling – maybe we shouldn't even think about it now. They must be waiting for us in Oregon."

"Yeah," he said absently. "Wonder what happened farther inland?" He herded the *Latecomer* down along the border of Lakes Ontario and Erie. Cleveland was dotted with lakes, the city rubble choked with brush. On a zigzag course, Detroit was a wilderness, Chicago almost a part of Lake Michigan. Carol's spirits sank with each revelation.

They arced high above the jet winds, on course to Oregon.

Ken almost shouted with joy when their beacon code came in weakly, strengthening as they approached the Pacific. Carol hugged him until he relinquished control to the autopilot and gave her his undivided attention.

The chronometer ticked away time, but Sol gave up the unequal race, and so it was another morning of the same day when Ken slipped the *Latecomer* over the mighty Cascades, homing on the beacon until they both saw the outline of a long, level, arrow straight runway carved from forested mountainside and spanning chasmal, growth-choked gulches.

But it was the outline only, discernible through a light rain. "At least two years' work," mused Ken, "littered with at least a hundred years' debris. *And we've only been gone a day.*" He killed signal reception, circled the runway.

Carol pressed his arm. "It's been longer than a day, Ken. I mean, we've actually used up more time, because it was morning when we were over New York, and it's still –"

"Okay – day and night don't mean much. But we've clocked a little over thirty-three hours since we took off. That's *our* time."

There was a catch in her throat. "I know, darling. Something's horribly wrong. Everybody we know must be dead!"

His jaw set, then he said gently, "Snug down, kitten, we're going in."

She glanced through the port. "But how can you land on *that?*"

He tightened the couch about them. "Blow the stuff out of the way," he said cheerfully. "Maybe." He swooped in from the east. "Keep an eye peeled for the Caves' entrance – I bet it won't look like it did last month."

The *Latecomer* touched the runway at little more than a hundred miles per hour. Its forward rockets braked sharply, blasting aside the scattered dead limbs and smaller trees – roaring, bucking and hissing. Its underside buckled from triphammer contact with rock slides and a few larger logs. It grated to a bumpy halt, gouged, scarred, split, its warped hull a forever useless thing.

Before opening the port he buckled the long knife at his waist, had Carol do the same with the short one. He climbed out, breathing deeply of the warm, moist air, savoring the incense of pine while helping Carol to the ground.

They avoided the radioactive path made by the ship, picked their way along the side of the strip until Carol pointed and cried, "There it is!"

Ken gripped her arm. "You follow behind me, and if the welcoming committee moves this way you get up in that big madrona over there."

"What?"

He pointed out the bear, watching from a wet tangle of brush. "If it's a male – or a female with no cubs – we're probably all right."

"Oh. But what will *you* do?"

"Don't argue, Lieutenant." His hand moved to the pommel of his knife. Ranger training wasn't exactly qualification for tangling with a bear, but long odds were becoming commonplace.

The animal remained where it was. They climbed over a rock slide and faced a wide bronze door protected by a concrete foyer. Out a way from the door was –

"Look, Ken – that's been a recent campfire!"

He whipped the blade from its sheath. "C'mon, kitten – get that knife out!" He vaulted the ashes.

A six-inch square was cut deeply in the dense metal. Ken poised his knife over a slot, and as Carol plunged her blade into the wall he rammed his home to the guard.

With a squeak and a sigh the door, terraced like a vault portal, swung outward slowly. Ken grabbed a recessed knob to hurry it up. Lights flashed inside, flooding a man-changed interior.

He leaped across the raised threshold, dragging Carol with him, swung the door shut and shot home two great bolts on its inner surface. On a rack just beside the door was an automatic rifle, ready for instant use. The psychologists had not known about the campfire, but they had planned for the possibility of a hostile builder.

Ken and Carol looked about the first of the labyrinthine caverns. Squared walls were lined solidly with glass-enclosed bookshelves stretching as far as they could see. Crowding the floor were machines, cabinets of tools, implements, instruments, weapons and medical and surgical supplies.

They moved to stand before a large video screen set near the door. Ken flipped the single toggle below it. A scene grew, showing a white-haired army colonel seated behind a desk, facing them.

"Ken – it's Dr. Halsey," Carol whispered.

"*Was* Dr. Halsey," said Ken heavily. "I used to wonder if we had the same instructors."

The officer's lips moved. "Hello, Ken and Carol. I've been selected to make this film to greet you, and I know both of you will return to see it." His eyebrows lifted in the quizzical expression they knew well. "I'm going to rattle off a lot of explanations and suggestions, but I imagine the first thing you'll want to know is how all the things you've seen could have happened so quickly. And knowing that, will clarify the rest.

"You remember the experiments the Air Force made, sending small animals above the stratosphere. By means of controlled diets and more complicated devices you'll find explained in a book, we learned that these animals were not subjectively experiencing the time-span they should have aloft. In effect, they were aging hardly at all away from gravity – the farther away, the less aging.

"We got some fairly accurate figures on the time-distance ratios. Briefly, assuming you held to your course until you were recalled, you can figure that an average of ten years has elapsed on the earth's surface for every hour you were in space."

Ken muttered, "We were actually out of atmosphere about twenty-four hours. That would make it the year –"

"About 2200," finished Carol breathlessly.

". . . how or why, but that Time was evidently a variable. The realm of physics was a madhouse – discreetly so, lest our enemies profit by our knowledge. There is no visual or other subjective means to sense the deceiving change in time-rate, or its illogical effects; we knew, for instance, that you would not see the moon as a solid ring girding a gyroscopic earth, as might seemingly be expected.

"Your message of recall was a record, slowed down to be within an intelligible range of fast chatter or slow drawl when you received it. We could have told you to open the envelope at a certain time or distance, but even minutes and miles were critical and" – the pictured features smiled paternally – "we knew your interest in each other might cause a delay, while" – the expression changed to serious sympathy – "we didn't know just when Space-Fear would strike."

Carol blushed and laid her cheek against Ken's chest. "They knew everything that would happen, didn't they? They – they *planned* everything!"

He crushed her to him. "Lucky they did, honey. Seems like they've put all their hopes in us."

". . . imminent war, and what radiation would do to surface life. We could not go with you, nor was there time to build underground installations for surviving more than half a century and emerging to a temporarily unproductive soil. We selected you to inherit the world, and you have had the hopes and prayers of your nation and your people."

They sat on a low chest and listened to the psychologist's voice for nearly an hour more. He finished on a message of hope. "You have seen the results of war. With the knowledge and material at hand, and the atmosphere craft waiting at the sealed exit, you can contact what survivors' descendants you may find in hidden corners of the world and lead them to the peaceful glory of Earth's future.

"Obviously, life will not visit back and forth between the stars, or even the planets. The laws of Space and Time confine man to one world – but it *can* be made the best of all possible worlds, free of war within, and free of conquest from without, since the reasons which keep man from visiting other spheres will keep other life from visiting him."

The screen faded and was silent, followed by a clear, trilling whistle which swelled in a paean of lilting sound. While Ken squeezed Carol's hand in mounting amazement, the piping strain formed clearly into words –

With understanding of universal laws, life may do as it wills, go where it wills . . . we have come to your planet to help you . . . may we?

The psychologists had not foreseen quite everything. . . .

www.ingramcontent.com/pod-product-compliance
Lightning Source LLC
Chambersburg PA
CBHW030416310726
48979CB00002B/437

* 9 7 8 1 4 6 3 8 9 9 0 3 5 *